T0197539

Miss Prissy

Donna E. Warren

To order additional copies of this book, contact:
Xlibris
844-714-8691
www.Xlibris.com
Orders@Xlibris.com

ISBN:	Softcover	978-1-6698-4779-3
	Hardcover	978-1-6698-4781-6
	EBook	978-1-6698-4780-9

Print information available on the last page

Rev. date: 10/04/2022

Miss
Prissy

Devora and James, 6-year-old twins, waited excitedly for their mother. They were going to a new store with a weird name, "Miss Prissy"! Mom said that they would learn new things and enjoy themselves while there.

"Ready to go to Miss Prissy," their mom asked as she walked up behind Devora and placed her hands on her shoulders.

"Yes, they both shouted and headed out the door.

"Not so fast!", mom said. "We need umbrellas".

"Umbrellas", the twins shouted. "It's not raining".

But it's hot outside and the umbrellas will shade us from the sun." said their mom.

"James, open the door for us, please."

"Yes, ma'am," said James as he ran to the door and opened it.

"Thank-you, James" said mom as she and Devora headed out the door.

"You're welcome" James yelled as he tried to beat Devora to the seat behind mom in the car on the left, Devora didn't like to sit on the right side, but.....

"Miss Prissy is not too far", said mom. "We are walking".

"I wish Dad could be with us", James said.

"You know he had to work, but he will meet us for dinner", said mom.

As they walked and sometimes skipped to the Shop, they passed the ice-cream parlor where Devora's favorite was chocolate and James' favorite was vanilla. They also walked pass the Pizzeria where they ordered pizza every Saturday night. James was in love with the cheese pizza, while Devora preferred the sausage pizza.

"Are we close" both twins asked as they came to the corner and stopped at a red light.

"Yes" said mom. "When the light changes, we will cross the street and the second shop will be Miss Prissy".

When they arrived at the Specialty Shop, called so because it was a store that specialized in Good Manners, mom held the door as the twins ran in and then stopped.

"Thanks, mom" they said and in the same breath, they said "Wow" and looked around the shop.

The wall was decorated with colorful banners that said:

- "Sorry"
- "Please"
- "Thank-you"
- "Excuse me"
- "May I"
- "Yes ma'am, No ma'am, "Yes sir" and "No sir"
- "Hold the door for others"
- "Hello" "Good-bye"
- "Good morning", "Good Afternoon" "Good Night"

There were so many colorful signs, so many people, so many tables and books that it was amazing. There was even a banner on cell phone use!

A young man walked up to us, introduced himself as greeter Mr. Thomas and told them about the shop. He said having good manners means learning how to express yourself with the utmost(greatest) respect, politeness and proper conduct. Each table has a card with a "good manner" on it and a description. Then there are opportunities where this "good manner" can be used. "Walk around and enjoy yourself. If you have questions, ask anyone wearing a "Good Manners" apron like mine." Before you leave, you will receive a card that you check off as you use the good manner during the next 2 – 3 weeks. Bring it back for a treat."

"Where should we start?" asked mom.

"Here, here", the twins said as they ran toward a table.

"Don't run, walk," said mom. "You may fall, or bump into someone".

Their first table had the words "Can I" and "May I" in card holders on the table. There were question marks all over the table.

"What's the difference," James asked.

"Read the card on the table," said mom.

James picked up the card and read: Can I means am I able to do it while may I means do I have permission." "What???"

"May I means do you have permission to get a cookie, go next door, etc. while 'can I' means are you able to do something like get a cookie or go outside."

"May I go to the restroom" is better than "Can I go toe the restroom." One talks about permission while the other talks about the ability to."

"Oh" both children said.

On the table was a book entitled "I forgot to ask you". Mom read a few pages to us. We discussed what she had read.

"Let's move on to another table," said mom. "I choose."

"This table looks fun", said mom as she walked toward a table that had "Yes ma'am", "Yes, sir" and "No ma'am", "No sir" in card holders on the table. The table was covered with a beautiful variety of flowers. A sign stated that the variety of flowers stood for the variety of people and ages we meet.

"You remind us to say this ALL the time," said Devora. "Right", echoes James.

"Let's read the card", says mom.

Devora picks up the card and reads, "To say "yes, ma'am, no ma'am, yes sir and no sir" is just polite. It offers respect to older adults. Some people may feel old if you say "yes ma'am, no sir, etc. If so, they have the right to ask you not to respond in such."

"I was taught to say yes ma'am, no ma'am, yes sir and no sir." said mom and I still say it as a sign of respect to older person. "Many people say it as a sign of politeness and respect. Read the other card"

James picked up the card and read, "You may simply say "yes", "no", 'of course", etc. to answer a closed-end question, but do not say it with an attitude."

"What does that mean?' asked James.

"Attitude means to answer with a roll of the eyes or answer in a resentful (not nice) way," said mom.

The book on the table was entitled "Yes ma'am". She read us a few pages from the book, we discussed what she read and then moved on.

"Wow" said mom, glancing at her watch. "It's getting late. We need to meet dad for dinner. ONE MORE TABLE. We will have to come back."

"Look at this table! There are three card holders!!!!" Wow! The table was covered with clapping hands and balloons. The cards in the holders read: Please", "Thank-you" and "Excuse Me".

"Read the card".

Devora read the card." You say "please" to be respectful and to politely ask or request something. You say "thank you" when you appreciate what someone has done or said. You say "excuse me" when you need to get attention or if you need to interrupt someone or walk in front of them. You also say, "excuse me" when you sneeze, cough or burp in front of someone."

"Wow! the twins said. "So much information!"

The book on the table was entitled "Social Story Sayings" and talked about the manners that were listed on the card. Mom also read a few pages from the book to us, and we discussed what she read.

"We need to go," said mom. She stopped at the front desk, talked to another greeter and picked up a check- off card for us. We were also given a pamphlet on Good Manners and its importance.

"Please come back again", he said.

"We definitely will," say mom. "There's so much they need to learn and understand."

"What about our treats?", the twins asked.

"Your mom has the check-off card. Complete it and bring it back." What's our treat? "It's a surprise he said as we headed for the door.

"We must remember that good manners help us feel better about ourselves and help build healthy attitudes and relationships," mom said. "The right conduct helps with building a nice personality and helps us communicate, to others, that you care about them."

"Let's get home so we can go have dinner with Daddy."

Printed in the United States
by Baker & Taylor Publisher Services